SCRUFFY BEAR
and the LOST BALL

Chris Wormell

A Tom Maschler Book
Jonathan Cape • London

One day a red ball
came flying through the
air towards Scruffy Bear.

So he kicked it.

It flew straight up in the air and disappeared among the branches of an oak tree. Scruffy Bear waited for the ball to come down. But it didn't.

Just then four rabbits appeared.

 "Have you seen our ball?" they asked.

 "Ball?" exclaimed Scruffy Bear. "Was it a red one?"

 "Yes," said the rabbits, nodding. "A shiny new red one!"

"Oh . . ." said Scruffy Bear, a little guiltily. "I think it may be up in this tree."

They all looked up, waiting for the ball to come down. But it didn't.

"Must be caught among the branches," suggested Scruffy Bear. "But I'll soon get it down – I'm an excellent tree climber!"

Actually Scruffy Bear had never climbed a tree in his life. It was much harder than he thought, and when he'd only gone a little way up, the ground looked a very long way down.

The rabbits were joined by six
white mice, and they all looked up
at Scruffy Bear, balancing on a branch.
"What's that?" called one of the rabbits. "I can see
something red among those leaves over there!"
Scruffy Bear saw the red thing too, and inched his
way along the branch, being careful not to look down.
He reached over and was about to grab the red
thing when . . .

"OI! What are you doing?" demanded Squirrel. "Leave my tail alone!"

Scruffy Bear got such a shock, he very nearly fell off the branch. "Sorry, I was looking for a ball," he explained.

"I'm not a ball!" snapped Squirrel. "No, you're nothing like one," agreed Scruffy Bear, climbing back along the branch.

A little higher up, Scruffy Bear found a hole in the trunk.

"The ball must have gone in here," he thought.

"Have you found it yet?" called one of the rabbits from below.

"Nearly," replied Scruffy Bear. He was just peering into the hole when . . .

"WHOOO are YOOOU?" hooted Owl, crossly. "Poking your nose into my bedroom! In the middle of the day toooo!"

Poor Scruffy Bear got such a shock, he rolled right over backwards and nearly fell off the branch!

"Sorry," he said, quickly climbing further up the tree.

Up and up he climbed, and
now he was so high he could
no longer hear the rabbits or
the mice, or even see the ground
down below. He felt a bit giddy.

At the very top of the tree
he found a great nest of sticks.
"That ball must be in here for
sure," he thought, and was just
about to peep into the nest
when . . .

"THIEF! THIEF!" squawked a huge bird with a long sharp beak. It was a stork. "You're after my eggs, aren't you!"

"No, I'm not!" protested Scruffy Bear. "I'm after a ball."

"A ball? There are no balls here, only eggs."

"Are you sure?" asked Scruffy Bear. "How many eggs do you have?"

"Why, four of course! I can count, you know!"

"You have five now," said Scruffy Bear. "And one of them is red."

"RED!" cried the stork. "That's not my egg!"

"No, it's my ball," said Scruffy Bear. He was just picking up the ball when one of the stork's eggs began to crack and . . .

. . . out popped
a baby stork!

This time
Scruffy Bear
did fall!

Down . . . . .

Down . . . . .

Down . . . .

Faster
and faster
and faster!

And when he reached
the ground . . . .

He bounced!

"Thought I'd come down
         the quick way," he said,

as he bounced again . . . and again . . . and again . . .

That afternoon they all played a game of football:
Scruffy Bear and the six white mice against the rabbits.

The rabbits won,
24 goals to 23!

For Jill

SCRUFFY BEAR AND THE LOST BALL
A JONATHAN CAPE BOOK 978 0 857 55011 8

Published in Great Britain by Jonathan Cape,
an imprint of Random House Children's Publishers UK
A Random House Group Company
This edition published 2013

1 3 5 7 9 10 8 6 4 2

The Random House Group Limited supports The Forest Stewardship Council® (FSC®), the leading international
forest certification organisation. Our books carrying the FSC label are printed on FSC®-certified paper. FSC is the
only forest certification scheme endorsed by the leading environmental organisations, including Greenpeace.
Our paper procurement policy can be found at www.**randomhouse**.co.uk/environment

RANDOM HOUSE CHILDREN'S PUBLISHERS UK
61–63 Uxbridge Road, London W5 5SA

www.**randomhousechildrens**.co.uk
www.**randomhouse**.co.uk

Addresses for companies within The Random House Group Limited can be found at: www.randomhouse.co.uk/offices.htm
THE RANDOM HOUSE GROUP Limited Reg. No. 954009
A CIP catalogue record for this book is available from the British Library.
Printed in China